30 Days-Streams of Consciousness
Book 3
Abduction
Lucinda Moebius

# 30 Days-Streams of Consciousness
# Book 3: Abduction

Copyright ©2016 by L.E. Moebius

Haven Novels 2011
Haven Novels
www.mywritersplace.com
First Hardcover Edition: 2016
First Paperback Edition: 2016
First E-Book Edition: 2016
The characters and events portrayed in this book are fictitious. Any similarity to a real person, living or dead is coincidental and not intended by the author.

**30 Days-Streams of Consciousness: Abduction**

a novella by L.E. Moebius. -1st. ed. p.cm.
ISBN-13:9780692706299
Cover design by Lucinda Moebius
Printed in the United States of America
**Haven Novels**

# Introduction

Stream of consciousness refers to the practice of writing down ideas as they come into your head. The conventions of grammar and appropriateness of language is usually ignored when using this literary technique. For those of you who cringe at the misplaced metaphor, or the comma splice, or the occasionally correctly spelled wrong word so frequently seen in this day of spell-check reliability, don't worry there are a lot more things in here to worry about. Concern yourself with where you are and who might be watching you as you go about your life. Wonder if reality is everything it seems to be.

A word of caution to the easily offended: some of the topics discussed by the voices may not be acceptable in mixed company. When you deal with reality like this it is important to allow the voice freedom.

# The Encounter

April 1st, 2016. The subject of this study is a young female, approximately 19 years of age by the target population calculations. Her full-time occupation is listed as student but her employment is that of what is called a waitress. This profession is unheard of in our society. To allow oneself to be in servitude of another is a great honor and to ask for any kind of reward would be of the greatest insult. The female calls herself "Beth". It is a shortened version of the name "Elizabeth" listed on the document giving the vital information dictated on the date of her birth.

We believe there is much to be learned from the observation of this subject. It is important the subject is unaware of our observations. There was a moment when we were almost detected in our observations. This subject's hibernation cycle is frequently interrupted by physiological needs. During one of the subject's frequent trips to the food preparation area of her abode she nearly spotted our observation recorder through the transparent openings in the outer structure. Fortunately, the technology was disguised to resemble one of the many toys the young ones frequently send into the sky. Perhaps she was concerned since the young ones tend to spend the majority of the hours of darkness within the structures of the familial units and the hour she awoke from her hibernation was during a time the young would not be playing.

In her culture Beth is considered a fully mature specimen, yet there is much about her behavior that reveals she is not quite ready for the responsibility expected of the adults of this species. It appears she is intelligent. She is able to expend the necessary resources to provide the necessary life-sustaining substances required to sustain her body. Since this culture does not provide the basic necessities of life for their population it is necessary for individuals to obtain methods of barter for items such as food, shelter, protective outwear and entertainment.

The target population has developed a system where they exchange items such as disks made of common metals disguised as semi-precious metals and rectangular shapes of odd colored papers in exchange for these items. Sometimes they use items representing these barter pieces in the shape of a rectangular piece of plastic with a series of numbers printed upon it.

For the most part the research subject diet consists of foods found in the section of her school categorized as the cafeteria. This facility produces mass quantities of sustenance claiming to be of nutritional value. Upon further analysis of the products produced within this facility we have discovered that while the products may have some elements of nutrients within them, the food preparers have added a mass quantity of what is qualified as 'additives' to the sustenance. The additional qualities of the additives do little to contribute to the overall health of the body and, on a grander scale, tend to prove harmful to the overall health of the individual consuming it.

One of the most unhealthful substances provided to the subject is classified as 'refined sugar'. Our study has shown this substance to be of the most addictive and harmful of the many elements produced by this subject's culture. We are in the process of trying to discover the appeal of this substance to the research subject since the only effect we seem to be able to observe is the addition of mass to the individual's body. It seems there is a moment of sensory gratification followed by a greatly increased energy output which is followed by a severe energy crash. It is puzzling for us to try to understand why this research subject would not only desire this outcome, but would choose to do this to itself.

Although we are attempting to understand the research subject by pure observation in its natural environment, there may be times when it will become necessary to bring the subject into the lab to perform experiments and take samples. Fortunately, other researchers have studied research samples from this population before so there is a precedence set for this subject. If we are careful we will be able to hide our presence from this population. We will have very little interaction with the research subject and have ways of deleting our presence from its conscious mind. We have high hopes this research will prove invaluable in our ability to someday find a way to safely interact with this species in the future.

Choosing this subject was not done lightly. We have sent many researchers into the general population to assess the population and to find subjects to provide a cross-population sampling. Beth represents many of the qualities we are seeking in a research subject. We hope this subject provides the answers we seek.

# Abduction

We had an opportunity to bring the subject into our lab and run a series of tests. It usually takes much more observation time before we find an opportunity to bring a subject into the lab, but the conditions were so favorable we had to take the chance.

The subject spent the greater part of the evening studying in the building commonly referred to as the library. She spent many hours using the inadequate equipment to research her companions' activities. It seems an awkward mode of communication. Posting ones' social activities on a website designed to limit in-person communication seems counterintuitive to the idea of being social.

Although the subject did spend a significant amount of time studying her peers' social activities it appears she spend time working on what she termed "homework". It seemed odd she was doing this work in the library even though the name deemed it as work required to be done at home.

The subject seemed to lack enough energy to return to her abode to sleep. Of course the companions who share her abode were having a celebration of some momentous event. Although we have been observing these subjects for a significant amount of time we still lack some basic understanding of the intricacies of all of reasons for celebration in this culture. This celebration seemed to be planned in order to celebrate an event termed "The Weekend". It is an event frequently celebrated, particularly by the young. Although Beth, out subject, frequently participates in these celebrations it seems this particular event held no interest for her. Perhaps her lack of desire to attend is directly related to the altercation with the individual she had chosen as a potential mate. Our observations did not allow us to ascertain what the altercation was all about, but it seems the male is no longer interested in pursuing the mating ritual. Of course, he may have been interested in furthering the ritual if there was any true pattern to the mating ritual, but it appears the attempt to mate varies from subject to subject. Even after the significant research performed on this culture we do not have a clear understanding of the mating rituals of these subjects. It seems life would be much simpler if we could introduce our method of mating to the population, but the rules of noninterference prevent us from providing the simple algorithm of assessing the mate on three areas of compatibility: temperament, intelligence and genetics. It has worked for us. My own mating has proven to be most satisfying, but as the researcher it is important to separate personal bias from data gathering.

When the subject's exhaustion overwhelmed her she entered a deep hibernation state. The caretakers of the library did not notice her when they closed the building for the night and she was left unattended. We sent one of our observers to see her safely home. It crossed the edges of interference, but we did not want to lose our research subject so early in the investigation.

The subject was in such a deep state of hibernation our observer was able to transport her to the lab without any interference. She will wake of from the anesthetic in her apartment. There might be some residual confusion since the substances used on her causes amnesia, but we are counting on the typical confusion due to the odd hibernation schedule practiced by these creatures. We were able to take baseline samples and implant a tracker under her skin. This will make it possible to track her activities and hear her conversations. We did not dare implant an external tracker since these devices are easily detected and this culture has violently rejected any attempt to observe or track their personal life.

We have high hopes for this research subject and look forward to the opportunity to perform many more experiments on her.

# Returning

It seems we miscalculated the subjects state of hibernation when we returned her to her abode. Although it seems she does not recall the experiments we performed on her, Beth has reported a vague sense of unease and what she classified as "bad dreams" to the individuals who share her abode. These individuals assuaged her concerns by explaining there were a number of substances mixed in the atmosphere of her abode and they explained the dreams were probably a result of inhalation of the substances when she returned from the library.

It didn't take much to convince the subject the events she described were the result of substance induced sleep. It is unfortunate she was exposed to the influences of the substances at this stage of the research since one of the reasons we chose this subject was she kept her body pure of false stimulants and depressants. Although her environment is frequently inundated by mind altering substances the subject rarely partakes.

We were able to observe the subject as she progressed through her day. Our concern for her state of mind grow as she traversed to each of her courses. She frequently demonstrated concern for her surroundings and continuously looked around as if expecting to find someone approaching stealthily behind her. It seems her experience in our lab has instilled a sense of paranoia in her mind and she has become uncomfortable in her environment. Our hope is that this feeling she has suddenly developed does not interfere with our ability to observe and record our findings.

The discomfort she felt during the day may severely impact our research. We will wait to assess the results from the samples we took before proceeding further in our studies. At this point we will continue our observations but we will wait to perform any more experiments until we assess the effects this round of tests had on her.

We do not intend any harm, but these subjects tend to be fragile in body, mind and spirit. It doesn't take much to harm them and our entire study will be for naught if we have to start our search for another test subject. We will allow the test subject a complete hibernation cycle before continuing our observations.

# Bruises

The marks on the test subject's body are remarkable. We noted the raised skin and abrasions from our restraints during our lab tests, but we did not expect these odd marks to appear so long after our initial study. It appears the past studies of these subjects neglected to mention the fragile nature of the outer coverings. We will need to analyze our restraints and assess ways to improve the experience.

The subject complained of discomfort and displayed the marks to her peers. We were fortunate to be able to use the test subject's subcutaneous implants in her ear and eye to observe her marks as she studied them in the reflective glass this culture seems so fond of using. Although most of the marks are barely distinguishable, there are a few dark, circular marks in her forearms and a mark about the size of one of her hands on her hip.

Her abode-mates encouraged her to receive help from one of her community medical establishment. Upon her arrival at the center she submitted to a number of tests similar to the ones we performed while she was in our lab. It was interesting to see her willingly submit to the studies we performed. If we would have known she was so pliant we would have just asked her to submit. Of course our lab looks significantly different from her cultures medical centers so we would need to spend a significant amount of time explaining everything to her and this would defeat the purpose of our observations.

We were able to easily obtain the results of the studies performed at the medical center. The record keeping of this population is surprising lax. The information is kept in data storage devices with codes easily deciphered even by the least intelligent of the researchers on my staff.

The notes taken by the staff at the medical facility are surprisingly thorough for such a primitive structure. In addition, we were able to find out some statistical data on the subject based on the measurement standards of the target population. Her height is listed as 5 feet 5 inches. Weight is 135, slightly high based on the standards of the culture, but her health is listed as over all good. From the actions of the young man who was taking her vital statistics it seemed she is considered highly attractive. When he left the room he surreptitiously looked at her address on the record. He does not appear to be a threat to her, more of what could be seen as a minor nuisance. It will be interesting to see this new mating ritual play out, if he chooses to pursue the subject.

Although the medical professional overseeing the subject expressed some initial concern over the marks on the subject's body she was able to speculate on possible causes without causing undue concern to her. Most of the tests performed by the lab came back well within normal parameters for what was expected for this subject. Of course, the tests are severely limited compared to what is available at our facility, but it is enough to obtain a baseline for what is expected in one such as her.

Although the medical professional was unable to confirm any diagnoses explaining away the marks on the subject's body she was able to correlate the memory loss the subject experienced with the timeline of the injuries. Explaining the subject probably experienced a fall or injury while intoxicated might have resulted in injury assuaged most of Beth's concerns, even though she did not recall imbibing any alcohol or partaking any narcotics.

Since we have obtained the records from the medical establishment we will continue our studies and compare our findings with these. If our memory manipulation of this subject continue to hold we will be able to continue our study. We do not want to cause harm to come to her. She seems to be a very fragile specimen.

# Memories

We were able to tap into our subject's memory cortex and retrieve a small quantity of data. The memory core of the research subject is quite different than too what we are accustomed. The information we found had been subjected to much modification. Surprisingly, the modifications were done primarily by the subject herself. The information was stored in random order and our attempts to retrieve it in an orderly manner met with some initial confusion.

The informational retrieval needed to be accomplished during the subject's hibernation cycle. It is necessary to perform this study during this time to avoid detection. We were able to use the implants placed within her mind to stimulate the memories and cause them to play out in her dreams. Since it was necessary to use the natural process these research subjects develop to process information it took some time to sort through the memories and separate fact from fiction. At this point we can only speculate what is imagined and what is real. It does appear she was attacked and bitten by a creature early in her childhood and it has caused an unreasonable development of a fear towards even the most diminutive of these creatures. Her fear does not extend to all four-legged creatures and she is frequently observed feeding and coddling a creature who appears to be more fur than anything and tends to make strange vibrating noises when satisfied.

We will need to continue to assess and categorize the memories we discover during the research subject's hibernation cycle. Perhaps by cross-referencing the information we gather from the experienced we observe we will be able to determine the truth from the imagined.

## Abduction Two

It became necessary to retrieve our subject and bring her to the lab much sooner than we anticipated. The implant in her right cerebral cortex was malfunctioning and it was necessary to bring her into the lab to extract the device and replace it with a new one.

Typically, a defective device would not usually cause concern, but this device seemed to be causing our subject some pain. As a result, she was dosing herself with a number of low powered pain relievers. The pain was becoming severe enough she was considering returning to the medical facility and seeking assistance and requesting substances to relieve the excessive pain. Although our devices are not detectable by the crude instruments at use in this cultures medical facilities, the medications do tend to interfere with their function. We had just started to tap into some of our research subject's higher cortex functions and we could not risk the contamination of the data. By removing the malfunctioning device, we were able to relieve her headache.

We were able to complete the subterfuge by creating a diversion at the far end of the college campus by providing one of the establishments with copious amounts of the liquid refreshment so desired at the celebratory events so frequent at the educational establishment. We knew our subject's suffering would prevent her from attending. Her abode companions did not concern themselves with her welfare and choose to attend the celebration, as we knew they would.

We were able to gain access to her abode and retrieve her from the nest she makes for herself during her hibernation cycle with relative ease. Of course one of our observers did allow the small creature to escape into the long narrow corridor outside of the main structure of the abode and had to spend a significant amount of time and effort retrieving the beast and returning it to the abode. Our subject appears to have an excessive attachment to the creature and we know if she lost it her grief might be as detrimental to the study as the debilitating effects of the pain relieving substances.

We were able to induce a deep hibernating state in our subject and replace the defective devices fairly quickly. We also recorded the marks on her body from our last encounter to assess possible methods of ensuring we did not leave this evidence behind again.

The return of the subject was much more successful than the retrieval. Our observers were able to ensure her creature remained in the abode as they returned the subject to her nest. Upon their return to the lab the observers expressed concern when they realized we had been replaying the events of the escape of the creature and subsequent pursuit throughout the research facility.

We have returned our attention to the research subject and will continue our observations.

The research subject does not seem to be suffering any ill effects from our minor procedure. She has been able to function throughout her day and has actually expressed regret to her companions for missing the celebration. She has also expressed the desire to visit the medical facility again to see if there is anything she could do to prevent this type of discomfort in the future. Perhaps this may be an excuse to experience the companionship of the care-giver at the center. We can hope this visit can provide us with more data on the mating ritual of this culture.

# Music

Arghhhh! For a moment there we were afraid our equipment was malfunctioning. The sensory input coming in from the new implant nearly shorted out our communication system. It took us a while to figure out the input coming in from the research subject was filtering in through devices she had placed in the sensory orifices responsible for her sense of hearing. The equipment the device is attached to must have been malfunctioning and set on its highest setting in order to create as much noise as it did. Our subject kept the devices plugged into her ears for the entire duration of her exercise regime. It was agonizing trying to filter the noise and analyze the physiological responses to the physical exertion she was placing on her body. If this is a routine she is going to maintain we will need to bring her back into the lab to adjust the settings on her implant. Why she would subject herself for such agony is beyond our comprehension. We much prefer the gentle sounds of the heartbeat and the throbbing undertone of our equipment than to the high pitched squeal of this noise.

In order to understand why the subject would torture herself with such a device we created a team to research the history of noise in this cultural subset. They have discovered the noises are called music and there are vast libraries devoted to sharing of the sounds with the public.

The research team decided they would need to analyze and study these sounds created by this culture and decided to do so by creating what is commonly referred to as "accounts" on the most popular of these sites. Hew they did so without having access to the research culture's monetary system is beyond our comprehension.

To preserve the sanity of our researchers we have created a separate work space for this team. They have been threatened with revocation of their research license if the noises emanating from their labs extend beyond the walls of their lab.

Until we understand more of our subjects habits we have decided to allow her to continue her routines without interruption. Our hope is she will refrain from using her devices to listen to music until we have a chance to adjust the settings on her implant.

# Marks

The marks on our subject's body are not fading as quickly as we expected. Perhaps our instruments are not designed to effectively gather samples from these creatures. We will need to visit their medical establishments and procure some of their equipment. They should be effective in gathering further samples. We will only need to use our equipment if we place more implants into her body.

It has been determined we will need to gather a larger research sample from our target population in order to garner the information we need. However, until we find a way to resolve the problem of leaving the physical evidence of our research behind we will need to limit our research to the currently chosen research sample. Perhaps using the target population's own medical equipment will resolve many of the issues we are having with leaving marks on the physical body. Then our only issue would be figuring out how to completely erase the shadow of a memory we leave when we work on the research subjects in our lab. It's too bad we cannot completely blend in with the population of the culture we are studying. Even the embedded researchers sometimes stand out in the form disguising their true selves.

There is a possible solution to increasing the target population study group, but it would involve gathering genetic samplings from the target population and creating a number of offspring to perform experiments upon. Although we have done this in the past with other cultures, this culture seems to value their genetic material as an extension of themselves and so unwittingly taking some undeveloped specimens to experiment upon might cross ethical boundaries. The committee will need to meet to decide if they are going to move forward with this plan.

I myself find the idea of growth and development in this species fascinating. I remember my own development as a time of safety and security as I formed in my pod, had my lessons broadcast through my informational portal into my core processing lobe and then finally emerging and taking my place as a researcher in this society.

To emerge as an underdeveloped, incomplete form from within the body of the female of these species and then being coddled, cared for and taught by those with greater skill and knowledge must be a frightening, yet exhilarating experience. The mark of the nurturer must be strong in this species since they choose to continue to repopulate themselves through these archaic methods. My own research has shown me our population used to procreate in this manner, although we have long since matured beyond this level of development. It makes me wonder what it would have been liked to be nurtured and taught and to be given a choice in my own destiny. My mate would never consider performing this experiment. It is satisfied with providing the genetic material necessary to produce offspring. Being responsible for their care and well-being may test its ability to focus and do its work.

I must delete this note in my report. There is no room for personal musing in scientific studies. I must be careful not to leave a mark in my records.

The subject has finally entered her hibernation cycle. I will see what her memories bring with her tonight.

Ah, she has decided to listen to a soothing sound of a beach with the call of the wild, flying creatures to lull her into hibernation tonight. Interesting.

# Being Watched

Our subject's behavior was completely out of character for her today. We have learned to anticipate her actions and have come to expect a certain routine as she works through her daily obligations. Although her schedule is not the same every day, she does tend to keep to a specific regimen. Today she decided to forgo attending one of her courses in favor of taking over the responsibilities of one of her coworkers. We are still trying to comprehend why he would forgo his duties in favor of taking what he termed "an Epic Road Trip". Our culture does not allow us to shirk our duties in favor of travelling with companions. From the moment we emerge from our pods we are relegated to the duty we were created to perform. To shirk from our duty would mean the end of our usefulness and as a result our existence would be terminated. It seems this culture values leisure time more than it values the individuals function in society.

While the subject was performing her daily exercise routine she frequently stopped and studied the region surrounding her. Her companion questioned her behavior and the subject explained for the past few days she had been experiences the feeling of being watched. Her companion attempted to assuage her concerns, but from Beth's behavior it appeared she remained unconvinced.

It seems we will need to warn our embedded researchers to be wary of our subject. It appears she has visited an establishment designated for providing defensive tools for those who might encounter danger as they progress through their daily routine. She has obtained some canisters or a pressurized substance that can cause some severe physical distress when released into the air near an individual's head. Although our physiology is not exactly the same as the subjects we are studying the genetic material we used to develop our embedded researchers is close enough that if they are exposed to this element it could cause some extreme discomfort. I will put it into my notes that it appears Beth has obtained an element classified as "pepper spray" and will warn the researchers to be cautious.

It is important our subjects remain unaware of our presence, but it seems this species has developed senses beyond the five most common elements. In all of our studies the research has shown the subjects have developed the senses of sight, hearing, smell, touch and taste, but some species of developed other senses as well. There seems to be an underlying ability to sense proximity, location, and emotional acuity. There may be other hidden senses in these subjects, but we will need to observe them closely to ascertain what they may be. I must be very cautious in my observations of my subject so she does not sense my presence.

# Bathroom

I must say the rituals of the research subjects are extremely fascinating. It appears they find shame in the simplest things and yet they are willing to describe these ritualistic events in the most public forum possible. The elimination of waste, the act of procreation and the cleansing of the body are completely done behind closed doors, yet the ritualistic style of mating is done completely in public. Events where individuals meet and exchange pleasantries in an attempt to gain a basic understanding of their hopes and dreams and plans for the future are discussed in open forums where food and beverage is served and music designated to cause unfortunate gyrations of various parts of the anatomy are all done in public. If music caused my body to do what some of these creatures are doing I would make sure it was all taking place behind the sealed doors of my research lab.

Why any being would feel it was necessary to hide behind closed doors to take care of such physical needs as to eliminate waste makes me question the vitality of this species. We understand the need to keep contaminates away from others, but this obsessive need to find someplace private to do so seems unhealthy, to say the least.

Our embedded researchers have also seemed to have difficulty with the concept of the outer coverings our target study subjects insist are necessary to their existence. It seems the theory behind these coverings is the need to protect oneself from the elements and offer some form of protection against harm. Since we exist in a controlled environment the necessity for outer coverings is unnecessary. It was difficult for our researchers to adjust to the temperature fluctuations of the study environment. In addition to understanding the purpose of the outer coverings, our researchers struggled with comprehending the symbolism behind each element of the outer covering.

It has taken us much more time than it should to understand the symbolism behind the outer coverings of these subjects. In addition, it appears the symbolism frequently fluctuates with the mood and attempt of the subject to assimilate into another culture. This has led to many struggles with adapting to the environment. It has also led to the accidental provision of levity in the lab as we reviewed the tape of the attempt at our researchers to work their forms into the coverings. Perhaps we should not have shown researcher forty-seven struggling to remove a garment referred to as "spanks" in the dressing room of a local provider of such coverings on the main viewer of the research center. Although the embedded agent was attempting to create a shape more pleasing to the study population it seems the struggle to remove the covering seems to be less than worthy of the effort. The researcher did leave the establishment with the garment so there must be some value to the struggle.

# Drawing

Our subject has taken to drawing her dreams now. It is interesting because we had never seen any type of artistic ability in her before. The interest and abilities of our research subject seem to grow with the passage of time. Trying to understand this culture is almost beyond our comprehension. The idea of being able to choose your own method of contributing to your society is as foreign as trying to change the shape of your head. We are designed with a certain subset of skills and ability. Our genes are manipulated so we can fit into the slot society has deemed necessary and we emerge from our cocoon prepared to take our place and function as society has deemed is necessary.

Our subject's latent artistic ability appears to have lain dormant for many years. It seems our initial studies and probes have stimulated areas of her brain and caused the talent to be thrust to the surface. At first she was rendering her sketches in a volume in which she utilized to write down important information from her courses, but now she has procured a volume specifically designed for the function of recording images sketched out by her own hand.

It is unfortunate we are only to study the artwork while she is working on it. She keeps the volume stored away when she is not working on it and we do not have access to her personal belongings we can only see the drawings through her implanted surveillance devices.

We are unable to ascertain the aesthetic level of the artwork since our culture's understanding or what is beautiful is so vastly diverse from our subjects' concepts. We cannot use the reactions of her peers as an assessment because she has not shared her artwork with any of them. She seems less than pleased with her endeavors and frequently covers her artwork with dark graphite.

I was fortunate enough to be reviewing the data recorded by her visual implant while she was working on her artwork before she entered her hibernation cycle. Much of her work consists of concentric images covering the page. It was difficult to find a pattern of images within the design. The only theme I could find was the image of optical orifices peering up from the page. At times the shapes of the orifices were reflections of her peers. There was some discussion about other images she created because the size and shape look more like the protective equipment we use during our research in the lab. It is obvious she is catching glimpses of the researchers as they are performing experiments. Trying to keep all trace of the research process from the subjects may be more difficult than we first anticipated. We must proceed with more caution as we move forward with our experiments.

# Fear

Our subject seems to be having some physiological responses to our study. This is an unforeseen side effect of our research. Although the physical marks have faded from her body, it appears there are some emotional scars she is continuing to carry with her.

During the hours of her hibernation cycle she frequently awoke and sat up, looking around the darkened room as if trying to ascertain if there was an individual in the room with her. It appears each time she awoke her body would release a surge of adrenaline causing her heartrate to significantly increase and her blood pressure to rise. The frequent episodes of wakefulness have left her with many physical side-effects. She had difficulty arising from her hibernation despite many warnings by the device beside her nest. Each time the device would create its loud noise she would reach out and strike at it until the noise was silenced. After a number of warnings, it finally stopped making the noise.

We observed her hibernating long past the time she usually arose to prepare for her studies. When she did finally arise it was done with great haste. The subject quickly changed from her hibernation coverings into her day-time garb. She did not take the time to perform her cleansing ritual before leaving her abode. Her pulse rate and blood pressure as she left her apartment were similar to the rate we recorded during her waking moments during her hibernation cycle. I wish I could have caught some glimpses of her memories during her hibernation cycle to assess if there was any correlation between the memories and the emotions she was experiencing as she left her abode, but the memories must have been buried deep within her subconscious mind because the implants could not access them.

The emotional awareness of these subjects speak to their primitive form. Our culture has evolved far beyond the need for emotional awareness and find the simple interplay of emotional subterfuge fascinating. Our subject appears to want to deny the emotions she is feeling and since we do not have a frame of reference to assess her emotional state we can only speculate what she is feeling. We have made an extensive study of the emotions of our subjects, but it is difficult to quantify such a unique concept. In addition to seemingly have numerous emotional reactions, the target population has many different ways to describe their emotional state.

For example, we have learned when one of these subjects are confronted with something that causes adrenaline to rush through their body and heartrate and blood pressure to increase they frequently use the following words to describe what they are feeling:

Fear
Anger
Love
Passion

Hate

Desire

Happy

Thrilled

Hot and Bothered (We think this is three words, but they are frequently used together so they may only have one definition)

Desperate

Mad

Pissed off

Excited

Turned on

We could add many more words to this list but we only have a limited amount of space in which to record our observation. Of course, these are just the words used in this particular research study's vocabulary. There are many other languages spoken in this particular study population. Fortunately, the groups who speak these different languages tend to cluster together so it is easier to find research samples. There is an entire lexicon available for each of the languages but since the research on this population started after I had emerged from my pod I did not have the opportunity to learn all the nuances of each language. It is much more difficult to learn new information after the memory synapsis are already formed. The future generation will have the knowledge of the language lexicons of these research subjects. It is too bad they will not resemble these species enough to fully integrate into the culture and learn about them through more than just observation and occasional studies of a few select subjects in the lab.

We have managed to procure quite a collection of medical devices used to perform experiments in this culture's research facilities. There are medications designed to render a subject completely unconscious and unaware. It is yet to be determined if this equipment will help us hide our experimenting on our subject.

## Abduction Three

Perhaps we were too hasty in attempting to bring our subject to the lab this time. In order to avoid detection, it is necessary to ensure she is alone before we take her to our lab. We had such an opportunity when she worked beyond her normal hours at the establishment where she serves nourishment. It was long after the hours of daylight and she was walking to her abode alone. Typically, she walks with a companion, but the hour was late and her companion had already left.

The researcher tasked with bringing her to the lab was able to render her unconscious quickly. We were able to maintain her hibernative state during the procedures. The medical equipment did make it easier to gather samples without leaving marks, but we are unsure of the function of some of the devices. Sometimes the limitations of our learning process can lead to frustration. There is great hope the future generation will be able to assimilate the knowledge of this target population and will be know the function of these devices. Unfortunately, the current pods are not set to hatch until long after the research study is scheduled to be concluded.

We were able to gather quite a few samples without having to restrain her or adjust her memory cortex. In order to assure our overseers this study will be successful we will need to keep our subject under close observation. We were able to add another implant just behind her right visual orbit so we will be able to ascertain her location at all times and will not need to have an embedded researcher following her. This should help alleviate some of the anxiety she was experiencing when we were keeping her under close observation.

The other residents of her abode had not entered their hibernation state when we returned our subject to her home. We had one of our embedded agents walk her to her door and explain to the others she had imbibed too much of the liquid served at the restaurant that frequently works to debilitate the partaker. This seemed to satisfy their curiosity over her impaired state. Fortunately, the embedded agent very closely resembles the current study group, at least well enough that if he wears a simple covering over his head, much like the individuals who like to ride the long, narrow piece of wood set upon wheels tend to wear, he can easily pass as one of them.

The companions of her abode assisted her in preparing for hibernation. There was some discussion about taking her to the hospital because her behavior was so out of character for her, but one of them said she would keep an eye on her since the companion said she had a paper due the next day and she needed to write it still. It is difficult to comprehend why an individual would wait until a task was required to be completed before starting it. Our conditioning gives us a sense of urgency and to delay working on a project would go against our very nature.

# The Ship

It appears we made an error in judgement. Our subject has been having some disturbing images forming in her cerebral cortex during her hibernation cycle lately. Even though we have attempted to keep her in her hybernative state, it seems she is much more aware of her surroundings in the lab than we calculated her to be. We have been able to capture some of the images before they fade into nothingness and they appear to be quite disturbing. I have filed the images away in hopes the overseers will not become aware of the findings. I do not want to lose the opportunity to continue our research study.

It is difficult to find useful data from such fragile subjects. Any changes in the status quo upsets their constitution. Casual observation has shown the subject's emotional state can actually affect their physical well-being. Our culture has eliminated most disease and we found it quite surprising to discover bacteria and germs still have debilitating effects on these subjects. We will need to balance the health and well-being of our subject with the need to gather data.

There are many images in our subject's cerebral cortex and it is taking some time to sort through them. Many of the images appear to be distorted, but some of them have come through very clearly. My face for one. I never enter the lab without my protective equipment so she must have seen me through the transparent barrier as I was donning my gear. The representation of my face is very clear and, quite surprisingly, accurate.

At some point during her hibernation cycle it seemed she thought of herself as being trapped in a long, well-lit corridor with doors lining the sides. She must have imagined she was being chased by some vicious creature because in her cerebral cortex she was running through the corridors and continuously peering behind her to see what was there. Her heartrate and adrenaline levels were higher than any we have ever recorded. Her level of activity in the night did not warrant her body's physical reaction. She did thrash about in her nest and struggle with the wrappings encasing her. At one point she awoke, sat up in the bed and cried out into the darkness. One of the residents of her abode must have heard the noise because she came in to check on her. By the time the other individual entered the room our subject had entered back into her hibernation. Her companion shook her until she arose, but our subject did not appear to recollect the image that frightened her.

We are having difficulty understanding the images in her mind. Although we transport her down long corridors to bring her to our lab, they do not appear to be the same type of corridors as we have at our research facility. Our lab is cordoned off from the rest of our facility because we do not want any contaminants entering our bio-facilities. Our subjects are never allowed to wander freely about our lab. They are always kept in hibernation and are only transferred through the halls on the exam tables. We have eliminated disease in our culture, but there is always the chance our research subject's culture may be carrying a viral infection we have not developed an immunity to as of yet. Although our passageways are brightly lit, we would never chase a research subject through the lab. We would release a neurotoxin designed to render them unconscious before sending in a retrieval team.

We will have to see if we can implant another recording device in our subject's cerebellum the next time we bring her into the lab. Perhaps if we place it closer to the amygdala we will be able to retrieve more of her hibernation images. Until then we will have to keep her in a deeper hybernetic state while we are performing experiments in our lab.

## Gentleness

I touched her. I know I broke protocol, but I needed to know what she felt like. Her skin was warm and surprisingly smooth. I shouldn't have removed my protective gear. I have probably exposed myself to more bacteria and viruses than my entire species has carried for three generations. It took me the remainder of my work cycle to complete all the necessary reports because of the touch. If the overseers knew it was deliberate I'm sure I would be up for termination. Some things are worth risking termination for, though.

Her body needs to be handled with such care it is difficult to move her and take the necessary tests with all our protective gear. I do not mean to damage her, but sometimes I still leave marks on her when I do my work. I know she does not feel any pain and we keep her deep in her hibernative state, but even as I worked on her moisture gathered in the corner of her occipital orifice and spilled out on to her face. I needed to wipe the moisture away and I couldn't do it without removing my protective covering. It was such a small piece of equipment I didn't think it would do any harm.

I will be spending some time in isolation while my supervisors assess if there is any danger to myself or others. Our lab is so isolated that even if I was exposed to illness I would be terminated and my corpse would have been destroyed long before the illness spread to the rest of our species.

I wonder what would happen to this research center if one of us did contract an illness. We are well-stocked and I have no concerns about our ability to survive if the project overseers decided to terminate our connection until the disease ran its course and all exposed researchers were terminated. It is not an issue discussed often because the idea of separating from the overseers, even on a temporary isolation protocol basis, might appear to be rebellion and no one in this research center would risk termination over such talk.

I know the overseers are interested in our reports on this society. The workforce potential of the population and the reproductive abilities show promise; however, they are such a fragile species it would be difficult to maintain their health. They also tend to have a stronger sense of self-identity and even though they do offer service to one another, there is an aura of independence that would make them a difficult species to control.

These notes will be destroyed. Termination is not a viable outcome for me at this point. We will see what the tests reveal during the next work cycle.

# Tests

I have been cleared to return to my duty station and to continue my research. There is no chance I will be spreading any disease amongst my research partners. The number of reports I needed to file because of a moment of weakness will put me behind on every test I need to run. I wonder if the moment was worth it.

I can still feel the warmth of her cheek against my flesh. The gentle give of her skin against mine and the pink flesh lightening to white and then back to pink as I applied pressure and released it. It took just the tiniest bit of pressure to change the tone of her skin. I wasn't surprised to discover our experimentation is still leaving marks on her body.

I am behind on my work. It is important I put aside these moments of wonderment. All I am doing is causing a delay in my work. There is some information I still need in order to complete my experiments. I must analyze the samples I gathered and prepare for the next round of experiments. This entry is short because I have much work yet to do.

# Sleep

Our subject's hibernation cycle is becoming more erratic. She frequently arises and traverses to the room designated in her abode for the elimination of bodily waste and self-cleansing. She does not spend a significant amount of time in there but the residents of her abode have noted the frequency and have made comments about the frequent trips. They have mentioned some possible causes for her frequent need to eliminate her liquid waste, but she has reassured them it is impossible since she is waiting for marriage. We are unsure of the meaning of the comment, but it is possible for her to be incubating another lifeform.

The overseers ordered tests to assess if these research subjects are genetically compatible with our species. We performed the tests the last time we had her in the lab. We will be able to retrieve any genetic materials from our subject the next time we have her in the lab. She won't even be aware of the tests.

I have been tracking our subject's hibernation patterns since we began these experiments. I have been curious about this concept since we first learned about it. The idea of spending nearly one-third of one's existence in hibernation is such a foreign concept it is difficult to understand why it would be allowed. Our overseers would have us terminated if we were to spend more than our allocated hibernation cycle in our regeneration pods.

I also am curious as to why she dreams. Dreams seem to be such a waste of brain power. Our minds are designed to focus on our tasks. Imagining a life outside of our function is far beyond our ability to conceptualize. I wonder what it would take for our kind to develop the ability to dream.

There is no reason for me to wonder and ask these questions. Our overseers would never allow us to dream. It would be a waste of time and energy. I would not even know where to begin a dream. I have no memories of my development before emerging from my maturation pod and my entire existence has centered around running tests and working in this lab. My dreams would be an endless round of taking samples and running tests.

Her hibernation cycle is also being interrupted by her dreams on a frequent basis as well. Her fears are creeping to the surface and interrupting her natural cycle. Her frequent interruptions have led to her need to hibernate at odd hours. If these is a defect in the species, I'm sure the overseers would not be interested in adding their genetic material to the work pool. They are already concerned about the streak of independence demonstrated by the research subjects. Perhaps they will pull us out of the research prematurely. I hope not. I would like to see this research through until the end.

## Abduction Four

Her body is so fragile it's hard to believe it doesn't break apart at every touch. Bringing her into the lab this time proved to be more challenging than we expected. We needed to assess the progress of the development of the fetus to assess when we can harvest it. Our superiors have yet to decide exactly how to proceed with the result of this experiment. It is doubtful our maturation pods will be effective for the development of this offspring. The pod is designed to accelerate growth and provide training and conditioning so by the time the individual emerges they are prepared for their role in society. The minds of these creatures are so complex there is some doubt to the ability of the pods to help the offspring develop fully.

We cannot allow our subject to continue to incubate the offspring for much longer. The blending of the genetic material has produced some interesting results. We are going to attempt to transfer the fetus soon, but we need to assess our subject before proceeding.

Her skin seems to lack some of the coloring it had before. This may be a result of the discomfort she is frequently feeling in the morning. The first time she violently expelled her previous meal into the bodily fluid waste receptacle we were concerned she was rejecting the combination of the genetic material. It appears the experiment was successful because the offspring is developing albeit at a much slower rate than expected.

We will not be able to return our subject to her abode in a timely manner. Typically test subjects are returned after only a brief time in the lab. According to our research the population here refers to the time period as hours or days. It is in our best interest to return our test subjects within a few of the time frame they refer to as hours. It is more difficult to keep the subject's awareness suppressed for more than that brief time frame. These tests will take a few of their days.

We were fortunate the research subject chose to spend her weekend at the home of her childhood. She did not give her family forewarning of her intended visit so we were able to intercept her at the station where she was intending to traverse across the city in the large vehicles referred to as a "bus". It took a significant amount of subterfuge to draw her away from the main building. I was greatly impressed with one of our embedded researcher's ability to mimic the injured creature many of our research subjects care for in their abodes.

I am working on an experiment to implant images in the minds of our subjects. It is similar to the technology used in the pods to implant knowledge in developing offspring. The intent is to replace the fearful imagery of her days here with some hopeful memories of a journey with a newfound friend. If this is successful it may have application in the development of the offspring in its pod.

The subject is starting to stir. I must carefully measure the risk of her awakening with her health and the health of the offspring. The overseers have made it imperative we do all we can to ensure the future development of the offspring as it may hold the entire future of our species. The importance they are placing on this experiment is odd, but it is not our place to question. We must follow the commands of our overseers or we risk termination.

# Family

I have been assigned the duties of researching the concept of family based on this culture. The overseers believe understanding the foundation of the family may bring to light concepts for caring for the offspring we are preparing to deliver. Our culture does not have the equivalent unit of family to base an understanding of this phenomenon upon.

My research has taken me back into the archaic history of our own culture to provide a framework for understanding this cultures familial units. The scope of this project may greatly outreach my ability to understand even the basic family unit. In our histories it has been reported that there were three recognized genders: Male, Female and Androgenic. The females were responsible for the bearing of children that was the mix of the male and female DNA. The male provided DNA to reproduce with a female. The androgenic gender was frequently born with the genetic make up of either a male or a female, but due to some unknown factor either felt they were the other gender or did not belong to either gender. They did reproduce, if they chose to do so, based on the gender they were born, but identifying their role in the familial unit was impossible based on historical records. The family unit has long been dissolved in our culture since the implementation of the pod used for development. Our kind are not "raised" by parents who care for us when we are to underdeveloped to care for ourselves. We still mate, for the express purpose of providing genetic material to submit to the overseers, but we do not cohabitate.

The core unit of the family in this study group seems to be a male and a female joining together to raise and care for young, but just as they seem to have multiple descriptions for naming their emotional states, they also seem to have multiple configurations for the creation of family. Although there is a large focus on a bond between those who share a genetic bond they do not always adhere to this standard. I have yet to determine exactly how these subjects determine what makes a familial bond outside of genetics. The decision to create a family seems to be completely arbitrary by any standards.

I much prefer the idea of developing safely in pods with all the knowledge and experience needed to perform our duties implanted into our minds. Deciding to care for someone based on a genetic bond seems unreasonable. You shouldn't have to care for someone just because your DNA says you must. Of course, to care for someone would require a capacity to feel strong emotions and our creators eliminated that flaw in our species long ago.

# Journey

We were unable to perform the procedure on our subject at our lab and had to bring her to the main facility. It was difficult to keep her sedated for the entire journey and I am afraid she was aware of more than we intended her to see. I could see the confusion on her face, but communication with her at this stage of the experiment would be detrimental to the study. We were able to return her to her hybernative state fairly quickly, but I'm sure the damage has been done.

The procedure was a success and we managed to harvest the genetic material. The offspring is currently in a stasis chamber for the return to our lab. The overseers gathered the data they needed from the experiment and have left the offspring in our charge. They left it up to our discretion to decide what to do with the result of the experiment. I have discussed the situation with the other workers in my station, but none of them have expressed any interest in discovering what will develop from the genetic material. Since the overseers have expressed a lack of desire to continue the experimentation on this species they have determined to complete their duties here and await another assignment.

I could not help but reflect on the fate of our subject and her offspring during my entire journey back to the lab. I considered the repercussions of re-implanting the genetic material, but the psychological and physical damage done in performing this procedure would have far-reaching effects on her and I could not subject her to such detrimental practices. Although these kinds of experiments have been done in many other cultures, I do not believe our subject would fair well from such a test.

Returning her to her abode was far more challenging than abducting her. She was gone for nearly three days without any contact with her family or her companions. Although I tried to replace her memories with positive ones, I fear I have failed. She has been unable to explain where she has been and frequently lapses into a confusing diatribe about bright lights and strange shapes standing above her. The companions who share her abode have expressed great concern for her and have determined a need for her to visit the hospital. They believe she has been in an accident and does not remember what happened.

Our subject is experiencing great pain and is bleeding heavily from her reproductive organs. I have reported her condition to our overseers, but they seemed unconcerned and feel this cultures medical personnel will be able to care for her. I desire to take her back to the lab and treat her condition, but I have been forbidden to do so on threat of termination. I will observe her and determine if treating her condition warrants being terminated over.

# Choices

My entire existence has been decided, determined and planned for me since the moment of my creation. The overseers chose the DNA that would determine my base characteristics and intellectual development. I was given an assignment as soon as I emerged from my pod and that has been the sum total of my existence. I have never been given a chance to ever make a choice before. My meals have been prepared based on my nutritional needs. My companions were chosen for me based on what we were designed to become in order to make sure society function. There has never been a need for me to face a decision before.

The idea of deciding what to do with the genetic material from our most recent experiment is causing me quite a conundrum. I cannot bring myself to destroy it so now I am left with the decision to either place it in storage and wait for the overseers to make a decision or try to place it in a development pod and see what happens.

I tried to discuss these options with the other researchers in the other researchers in my lab, but they have no interest in the outcome of any experiments I perform. They insist I destroy the material. I have taken the sample into my personal workspace and will keep it safe there until I make my decision.

# The Pod

The offspring has been placed in a maturation pod. For good or bad I have decided to give it the chance at life. Although it seems the offspring is adapting to the pod it appears there are some complications with some of the pod's secondary systems. I was able to adjust the settings for the hybrid DNA but I don't know how long the offspring will be able to develop in the chamber. The overseers ordered him to be given the same programming I received while I was maturing in my pod. As long as he completes his maturation cycle he will have the knowledge and skills as I do and he will be able to join me in my research. I discovered the offspring is male, an interesting aspect of the offspring of this culture. There is no way to create an androgynous offspring with the DNA of this species. These subjects take eons to adapt and evolve and I doubt the overseers have the patience to take all the necessary steps to manipulate the DNA sequencing of these species.

The pod is accelerating the growth of this offspring. It usually takes a period of nearly ten months to develop to the stage of being able to survive without the aid of its host. Even when the offspring has reached this stage in development it still requires constant care in order to ensure its survival. The pod will accelerate the growth of the offspring so it will reach the point of maturation to survive in just a few rotations of this species time frame of days instead of months. It will achieve full maturation in 30 of this species rotation of days. The overseers won't tolerate any variation from this cycle.

I am left to contemplate the fate of this offspring. If he had been left to mature at the normal rate of his species what would his future be? Would he be a researcher like me or would he choose a different path for himself? Half of his DNA structure was chosen from the stock DNA used to create researchers, but the other half is from a species designed to be self-guided and self-aware. My research has shown our species used to have this mind-set, before the overseers came.

The overseers may yet decide this species is worthy of their guidance and influence. I must return to my research to determine the future of this species and complete my report to the overseers. Our research subject has been admitted to a medical facility for treatment. According to the medical records we were able to appropriate she has been diagnosed with a disease referred to as "cancer" and will undergo treatment. If I were to be diagnosed with such a debilitating illness I'm sure I would be scheduled for termination.

# Hiding

The overseers have determined this experiment is a failure and has ordered us to conclude our research and abandon the project. We are to take the subject into the lab one last time and attempt to erase all signs of our experiments. It will be difficult to gain access to the subject since she has been detained in a medical facility due to her deteriorating health.

Before we started this experiment I had never understood the wildly varying emotions of the research subjects. Now, as I am faced with leaving this region and embarking on the next task I find myself at a loss describing what I am feeling. Yes, I am feeling. It is a strange to use words to express the emotions roiling through my being. I actually am feeling a physiological response to the ideas rumbling through my head. I am afraid my emotions have caused me to do something rash.

I am not in the research facility at this time. I have abandoned my work station and am now in danger of facing termination. I could not carry out the orders form the overseers in regards to the offspring. My emotional state would not allow me to destroy the life I have caused to develop.

The order came in late in my work shift and I barely had time to act before the next shift came in. I'm sure if I hadn't have completed the task as the overseers had ordered me to the next shift would have destroyed the offspring.

He had developed to the point he would be able to survive outside of the pod on his own, although he will still need someone to care for him. I cannot leave him in the care of the overseers for they will surely destroy him. I have disengaged him from all the connections causing his accelerated development and taken him from the research center. Although he is physically no more developed than a child of nine-months of age according to this cultures standards he has been given all of the knowledge and understanding of a researching in one of our labs.

He is completely self-aware and can articulate his understanding of the situation. I have explained to him, to the best of my ability, the gravity of the situation and I hope he understands he cannot reveal to this culture his knowledge and understanding of the world.

I have managed to disguise myself as one of the research subjects and as long as one of them does not attempt to gain a close look under the hood I have pulled up over my head I should be able to hide long enough to accomplish the task I have set out for myself. Hopefully, I can complete the task and make it back to the lab before I am discovered. I falsified the records to make it appear I have destroyed the offspring and am attempting to accomplish the task of retrieving our test subject for the final experiments. Hopefully this deception will suffice for an explanation of my absence from the test lab.

## Abduction Five

I see it in her face. She is afraid and broken. Even in her hibernative state there are fear lines carved into her features. The traces of the moisture from her visual orbs has left traces on her face. When our visual orbs leak fluids it's generally a sign of illness. I have attempted to force my orbs to leak fluid but there does not seem to be enough moisture in my eyes to force it to flow down my face.

This will be our last attempt at gathering research from this test subject. I fear there has been so much damage to her fragile body and even more fragile mind there is not much left to discover. The overseers have given up on finding any redeeming qualities in this species, but there is something...intriguing...about them. I wish we could stay longer, but the overseers are transferring our team to another site far away from here.

The embedded researchers will stay here and continue to observe in their limited capacity. They are so adapted to the culture they will have no problem adopting and living out their lives until they reach their natural culmination. I petitioned to stay, but there is no way I could have stayed disguised for the long-term. Eventually I would be discovered, perhaps even brought into their labs to be studied.

I wish I could fill Beth in on her offspring and the hope I have for his future. He is adapting well to his situation and knows it is best for him to act the part of an unassuming infant and living as one of the test subject. He is aware of our test subject and the role she had in his creation, but understands if he tries to seek her out and explain his existence he may cause her fragile mind to slip even further into the abyss.

I do not desire to cause her any more suffering. Our studies have caused too much harm as it is. We have cured her injuries caused to her body, but the damage to her mind may be irrevocable. I have tried to excise the memories or our experiments from her mind, but I doubt my efforts were any more successful this time than they were in the past. My poor Beth, how badly did I damage you?

Someday we may return to this research center and continue the studies we began here, when your species has become more adaptable to the role the overseers have in mind for you. I will not see this in my lifetime. We are long lived, but I will not live long enough to see the changes we have affected by our presence here.

We tried not to leave a trace of our presence here, but every time we stepped out of our labs or brought a subject into the lab we left some sort of mark: a trace of evidence, a memory, a glimpse into a new world. Whatever it was, I'm afraid it has forever changed the path this culture was on forever.

I question whether or not the change was good or bad. Surely, we have done more harm to Beth than we could ever imagine, but her offspring is strong and healthy and more intelligent than any creature I have ever seen. He may yet be the hope for a better future for these research subjects.

Then again, I have researched enough of this research subjects past to know this culture is not always accepting of things that are different. I hope I have impressed this knowledge upon the offspring effectively. He needs to be able to hide away his differences so the others can accept him as one of them. I fear for him, but I know he will be safer amongst the research subjects than here with me where he would face termination.

I must return Beth to her room at the medical center now. She is no longer in danger of expiring from the injuries she sustained from our experiments. I hope her mental well-being will be restored as well.

## Choices

I have to do this quickly and in secret. I need the child to know I did not abandon him. There is no way I can keep the things I did a secret. The trail I left is too broad and littered with evidence of my transgressions. If only we weren't watched every moment of our lives. Even now I can feel their eyes on me, peering over my shoulder, reading my very thoughts. Programming my every movement. I hate them. Is hate a strong word? I have learned so much from this research study, maybe too much.

The implants in our subjects are going to be destroyed before we leave and I want to make sure the child gets this information before we leave. I was able to tap into his cerebral implant and I will give him this one last message.

Child, always remember, I gave you life. I took you from a tiny bundle of cells and gave you knowledge and strength. No matter what happens to me, remember it was I who loved you. Yes, I love you. It is a word I did not understand until you came into being. It is the word that will lead to my downfall. I risked everything for you to have life and I regret nothing. You are my gift to the world. In you beats the heart of strength and knowledge of everything we began here.

If your mother would have known you I believe she would love you, too. She does not know you exist and yet in her I see a pain and suffering I could never believe an individual could ever experience. She does not know where this pain is coming from, but I do. I understand her. I know her heart.

Everything that is good in you came from her. She is kind and gentle and sweet and loving. She is everything you would ever want in a mother. I am glad I found a safe place to deliver you. Already they have found you a home with loving parents. They can give you the safety and security I can't.

Despite what happened I will never regret giving you life.

I must end this now. They are coming for me and I must send this message while I have the chance.

# Termination

There is nothing more I can do for myself or the others. I have brought this upon myself. The overseers claim I have become emotional unstable because of my physical contact with the research subject. Despite my best efforts to hide my afflictions I have been discovered. The only redeeming quality I am finding in all of this is they have not discovered what I have done with the child. His very existence is buried deep in the achieves of his new life. To try to find him now and destroy him would create too many questions and the overseers try to avoid as many questions as they can.

I have been removed from the lab and am now locked in a cell while I await my fate. The overseers want to complete the dismantling of the lab before sentencing me for my crimes. There is still much work to do and my refusal to help them has caused an excessive work load on the others.

I'm sure they will want to assure my fate will be an example to others. Even now they have ordered me to write a confession to be shared with my workmates. It will be used as a warning for others who may be tempted to break the laws of research by allowing emotions to be released when studying a subject.

I do not know what words to use in my confession. Should I say I am sorry for my crimes? I do not feel sorrow. I do not know if others would understand the concept of sorrow. Sorrow is an emotion and the others do not feel emotion.

I am not sorry for what I did. This research has shown me what it means to feel and understand compassion. I can never be sorry for that. Should I be afraid? No, I know what my fate will be. I go to the termination chamber with a clear conscious. I committed a crime. I will be terminated. Beth's child will live. My destiny has been fulfilled.

## About the Author

L. E. Moebius is a pseudonym for Lucinda Moebius. Lucinda has been a writer since she was a child and was first published in 2010. Since then she has worked hard to create unique visions and stories. Her work includes novels in multiple genres including: Science Fiction, Fantasy, Paranormal, Children's Books, Screenplays and Non-fiction. Lucinda has a Doctorate in Education and loves teaching, but her greatest desire is to help others understand how literature and writing can bring enlightenment and understanding to everyone. She offers book coaching and advice to everyone, whether they want it or not.

Website: www.mywritersplace.com

Other books by Haven Novels
Echoes of Savanna: Book One: The Parent
Generation
Raven's Song: Book One: T1 Generation
Write Well Publish Right
Feeder: Chronicles of the Soul Eaters Book 1
30 Days Stream of Consciousness V. 1
30 Days Streams of Consciousness Vol 2: A Haunting
Children's Books:
Oh Brother!
Raising Grandpa